WAHL
(green)
MAR06

THE
ENCHANTED
SLED

To Chiara & her parents Milena & Michael

J.W.

To Salome

M.F.

Illustrations copyright © 2005 by Monique Felix

Text copyright © 2005 by Jan Wahl

Published in 2005 by Creative Editions, 123 South Broad Street,

Mankato, MN 56001 USA.

Creative Editions is an imprint of The Creative Company.

Designed by Rita Marshall.

Printed in China

Library of Congress Cataloging-in-Publication Data

Wahl, Jan.

The enchanted sled / by Jan Wahl; illustrated by Monique Felix.

Summary: Illustrations and rhyming text extol the joys of a

wondrous sled ride.

ISBN 1-56846-187-9

[1. Sledding-Fiction. 2. Stories in rhyme.] I. Felix, Monique, ill. II. Title.

PZ8.3.W133En 2004   [E]-dc22   2003061746

First Edition

7 6 5 4 3 2 1

THE
ENCHANTED
SLED

written by Jan Wahl & illustrated by Monique Felix

Creative Editions

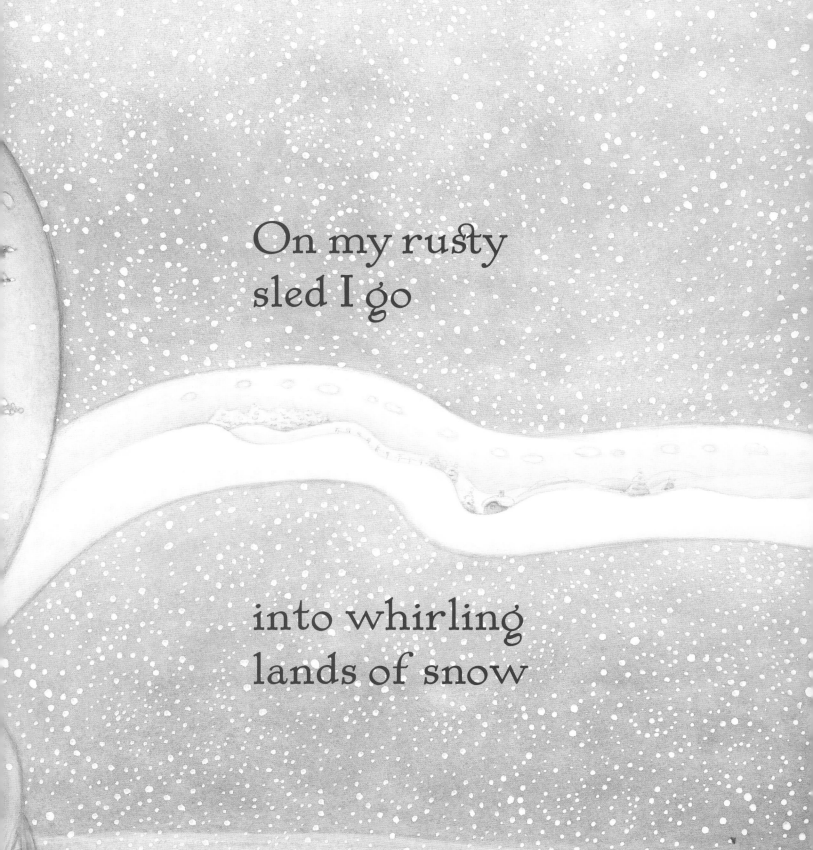

On my rusty
sled I go

into whirling
lands of snow

past crystal castles
high on hills

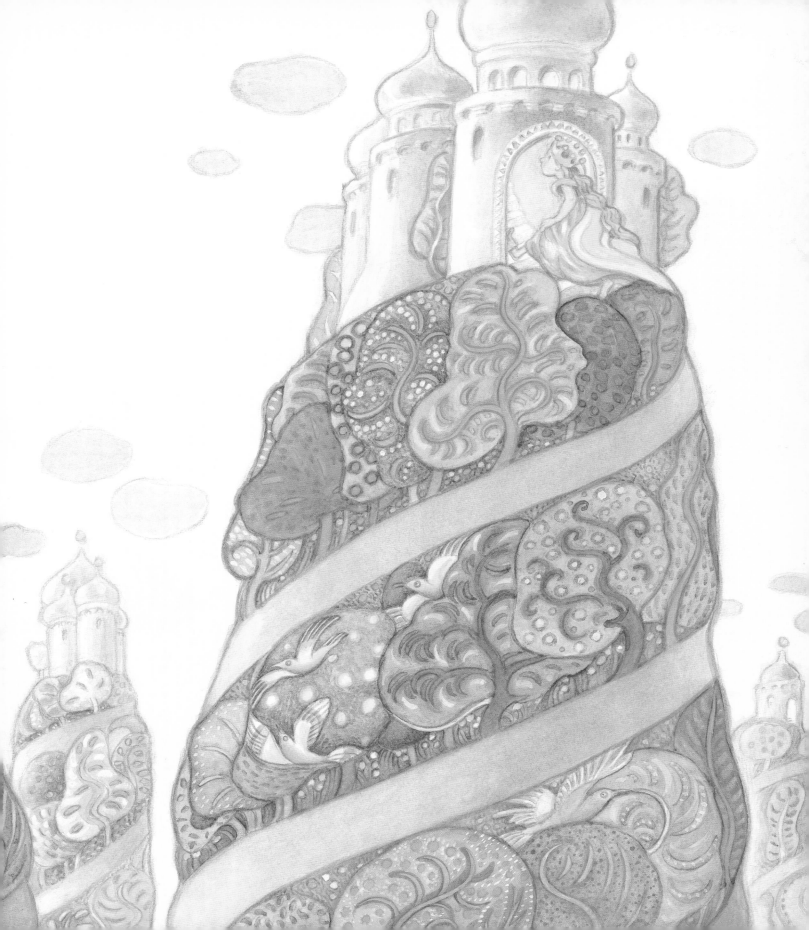

where long-legged soldiers

march and drill

where I become
a puffed-up toad

racing mice
down a winding road

where I can sail
on ribbons of air

and like a queen
I ride my chair

with the birds
I share the breeze

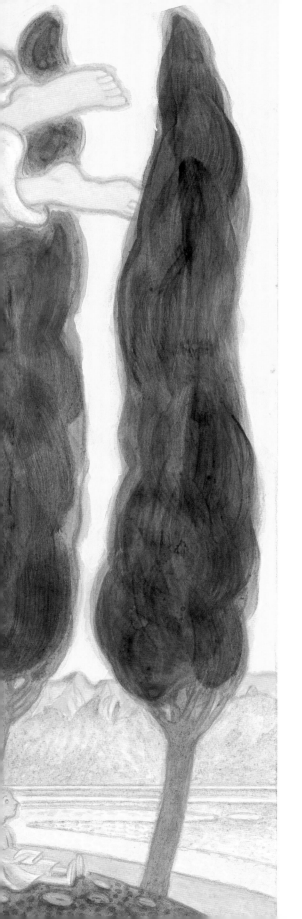

tipping over
the tops of trees

where the moon
becomes a lamp

and I'm a gypsy
asleep in camp

where I can watch
sun shining new

now I can be
invisible too

where the clouds
and I are one

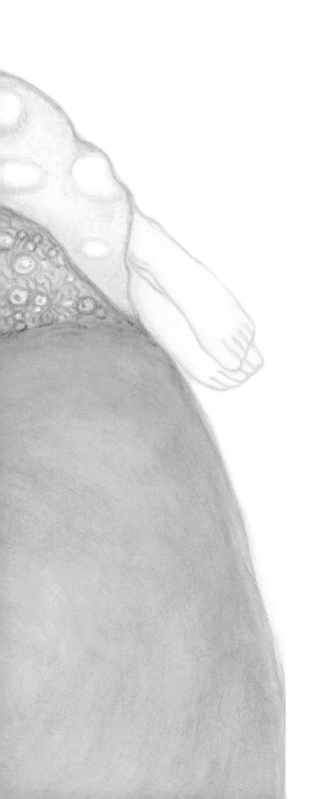

there my journey
is gently done.